Rapunzel

Book & Lyrics by Kristin Walter
Music by Michael Walter

Baker's Plays
7611 Sunset Blvd.
Los Angeles, CA 90042
BAKERSPLAYS.COM

NOTICE

This book is offered for sale at the price quoted only on the understanding that, if any additional copies of the whole or any part are necessary for its production, such additional copies will be purchased. The attention of all purchasers is directed to the following: this work is fully protected under the copyright laws of the United States of America, the British Commonwealth, including Canada, and all other countries of the Copyright Union. Violations of the Copyright Law are punishable by fine or imprisonment, or both. The copying or duplication of this work or any part of this work, by hand or by any process, is an infringement of the copyright and will be vigorously prosecuted.

This play may not be produced by amateurs or professionals for public or private performance without first submitting application for performing rights. Licensing Fees are due on all performances whether for charity or gain, or whether admission is charged or not. Since performance of this play without the payment of the royalty fee renders anybody participating liable to severe penalties imposed by the law, anybody acting in this play should be sure, before doing so, that the Licensing Fees has been paid. Professional rights, reading rights, radio broadcasting, television and all mechanical rights, etc. are strictly reserved. Application for performing rights should be made directly to BAKER'S PLAYS.

No one shall commit or authorize any act or omission by which the copyright of, or the right to copyright, this play may be impaired. No one shall make any changes in this play for the purpose of production.

Publication of this play does not imply availability for performance. Both amateurs and professionals considering a production are strongly advised in their own interest to apply to Baker's Plays for written permission before starting rehearsals, advertising, or booking a theatre.

Whenever the play is produced, the author's name must be carried in all publicity, advertising and programs. Also, the following notice must appear on all printed programs, "Produced by special arrangement with Baker's Plays."

Licensing fees for *RAPUNZEL* is based on a per performance rate and payable one week in advance of the production.

Please consult the Baker's Plays website at www.bakersplays.com or our current print catalogue for up to date licensing fee information.

Book and Lyrics Copyright © 2010 by Kristin Walter and Manhattan Children's Theatre
Made in U.S.A.
All rights reserved.

Cover Illustrations by Goopymart

RAPUNZEL was first produced in April, 2005 at Manhattan Children's Theatre. It was directed by Bruce Merrill, with set design by Leigh Henderson, costume design by Brad Scoggins, lighting by Brian Patrick Byrne and props by Mary Malmquist. The cast was as follows:

MOTHER..Elisha Allison

FATHER...Gershon Levy

WITCH..Holland Taylor

DANIEL...Adam Cooley

NURSE..Gershon Levy

RAPUNZEL...Sonia Hoffman

RENTAL MATERIALS

An orchestration consisting of **Piano/Vocal Scores** will be loaned two months prior to the production ONLY on the receipt of the Licensing Fee quoted for all performances, the rental fee and a refundable deposit.

Please contact Baker's Plays for perusal of the music materials as well as a performance license application.

CHARACTERS

Mother
Father
Witch
Daniel
Nurse
Rapunzel

SETTING

The play takes place in the parent's cottage, the palace grounds, the woods and in Rapunzel's tower.

MUSICAL NUMBERS

Be Strong (**MOTHER**)

I Know I'm Not a Prince (**DANIEL**)

Be Strong (Reprise) (**WITCH, RAPUNZEL**)

I Know I'm Not a Prince (Reprise) (**DANIEL**)

The Magic of Tears (**FATHER, MOTHER**)

Be Strong (Reprise 2) (**RAPUNZEL**)

I Can't Go (**RAPUNZEL, DANIEL**)

Witch's Song (**WITCH**)

The Magic of Tears (Reprise) (**MOTHER**)

I Know I'm Not a Prince (Reprise 2) (**DANIEL, ALL**)

Scene One

(A cottage in a small medieval village. **MOTHER** *and* **FATHER** *are admiring their newborn twins who are sleeping in a cradle.)*

MOTHER. They're perfect. They're just...perfect. Aren't they perfect?

FATHER. *(laughing)* Yes they are. At least as perfect as they were five seconds ago. Maybe more.

MOTHER. I'm sorry, I can't help it. I just can't believe they're ours.

FATHER. Two of them. I wasn't expecting that.

MOTHER. I should have known. There was too much kicking for just one baby. I hope they weren't fighting already – we'll have our hands full by the time they're old enough to talk.

FATHER. Look at them all snuggled together. I can't imagine they would ever fight.

MOTHER. They do look so close. I think they will be great friends when they grow up.

FATHER. They don't look very much alike, do they?

MOTHER. Well, it *is* a boy and a girl. I'd worry if they looked too much alike.

FATHER. You know what I mean.

MOTHER. I think the boy looks like you and the girl looks like me. *(sighs)* I could not be happier.

FATHER. Are you? Happy, I mean?

MOTHER. Of course. Why wouldn't I be?

FATHER. I was thinking about the witch.

MOTHER. Well don't think about it. We haven't seen hide nor hair of her in months. She probably realized how ridiculous she was being and went away. Imagine – all that fuss over a little head of lettuce.

FATHER. It was valuable lettuce, though dear....rapunzel lettuce.

MOTHER. Rapunzel, romaine, iceberg; I don't care what it was. She isn't coming back and I refuse to spend another minute worrying about it. Look... we have two beautiful babies to care for. What shall we name them?

FATHER. I've been giving that a lot of thought and I have the perfect names...Hortense and Clyde.

MOTHER. Please tell me you're joking.

FATHER. They're family names.

MOTHER. We love these babies. You don't name children you love Hortense and Clyde.

FATHER. Well, what's your idea?

MOTHER. I think we should wait a little. Let them tell us their names.

FATHER. How will they...?

MOTHER. Oh, they'll tell us when they're ready. *(to babies)*You're going to grow up big and strong, won't you? You'll be brave, and wise, and funny and smart. And I'll be there every step of the way. No matter what.

SONG – BE STRONG

BE STRONG
YOU'RE NOT ALONE
I WILL BE HERE BESIDE YOU
FOLLOW MY LIGHT, CHOOSE WHAT IS RIGHT
MY CHILD
BE STRONG

(There is a pounding on the door.)

MOTHER. What is that?

(more pounding)

FATHER. It's the Witch – I know it is!

MOTHER. It can't be. It's the wind, or a tree branch…

FATHER. It isn't the wind – it's her. She's come for the babies.

MOTHER. Don't be ridiculous. We're not giving her the babies.

WITCH. *(offstage)* I know you're in there!

FATHER. It's her!

MOTHER. Shhhh! If we're quiet, she'll go away.

WITCH. I know you're in there. And I want my baby!

MOTHER. I think she's serious.

FATHER. Of course she's serious!

MOTHER. I didn't think…How could she?…What are we going to do?

WITCH. I won't leave until I have my baby. *(crashing sound)*

FATHER. She's going to break down the door!

WITCH. Give me my baby! *(another crash)*

FATHER. That door won't hold forever.

MOTHER. She's not getting my children – I don't care how strong she is. I'll fight her if I have to.

FATHER. You won't win – she's too strong. *(another crash)*

WITCH. You can't hide from me!

MOTHER. Hide! We'll hide the babies.

FATHER. Where?

MOTHER. Anywhere. We'll go out the back door and run.

FATHER. She'll catch us.

MOTHER. She can't catch both of us. You take the boy; I'll take the girl. We'll go in different directions and run as fast as we can.

FATHER. I won't leave you.

MOTHER. You have to! *(crash)* Go!

*(She picks up a baby and hands it to **FATHER**.)*

Take him and go! I'll be right behind you.

*(**FATHER** takes the baby and runs off. There is an enormous crash, and the **WITCH** enters. The baby is between them.)*

MOTHER. Get away!

WITCH. Did you really think I would just go? We made a bargain.

MOTHER. You can't mean this!

WITCH. Did we or did we not make a bargain?

MOTHER. We did, yes, but…

WITCH. You stole my rapunzel. Your husband climbed the wall, came into my garden and stole my lettuce!

MOTHER. I was pregnant – I was having such cravings – I couldn't sleep; I couldn't think…

WITCH. And I sympathize. That's why I'm willing to trade.

MOTHER. That was lettuce – this is a child!

WITCH. We made a deal. I wouldn't go to the sheriff; you would give me your baby.

MOTHER. You can't have her!

*(She lunges for the baby, but the **WITCH** gets there first.)*

Give her back to me!

WITCH. You'll never get her back. Do you know where I've been these past months? In the forest, building a tower with no stairs and no door. That will be her new home, and you'll never find her. Ever!

MOTHER. No!

WITCH. She'll be perfect. My little Rapunzel.

MOTHER. Please…you can't…

WITCH. I can. No one can hurt me and get away with it. Not ever. *(She runs out the door.)*

MOTHER. *(running after her)* Come back! *(We hear the sound of horse hooves.)* Please, bring her back!

(FATHER enters, alone. He looks around the empty house.)

FATHER. Hello? Where are you? Are you here?

MOTHER. *(enters)* She took her. The Witch took our little girl.

FATHER. No!

MOTHER. I wasn't fast enough. I wasn't strong…

FATHER. You did everything you could. Don't blame yourself.

MOTHER. Where is our boy?

FATHER. I got as far as the well, and I saw a servant girl drawing water. I gave the boy to her.

MOTHER. What?

FATHER. I was afraid you hadn't gotten out in time – I thought I could help, so I just gave him to the girl for safekeeping. We'll get him right back.

MOTHER. Let's go! Quickly!

(They begin to hurry toward the well. The cottage disappears behind them and the well appears. As they run:)

We'll get our son, and then we'll go into the forest. The Witch said something about a tower. If we find the tower, we'll find our daughter.

(They arrive at the well. It's deserted.)

Where is the servant girl?

FATHER. She was just here. Where did she go?

MOTHER. Where is my baby? Did she leave him on the ground?

FATHER. I don't see him anywhere.

MOTHER. Who was she?

FATHER. I don't know. I was in such a hurry, I didn't really look at her. I just gave her the boy and said I would be back soon.

MOTHER. No…no! I can't lose both of them. Not both…

FATHER. We'll find them. *(He holds her.)* We'll find them. I promise.

MOTHER. My children…

FATHER. We won't rest until we find them. Be strong, my love. Be strong.

Scene Two

(The courtyard of the palace. **PRINCE DANIEL** *is alone, spinning a crown in his hands. He sings a birthday song to himself.)*

DANIEL. *(sighs)* Two hundred people at my party, and I don't know a single one of them. All heads of state and dignitaries. And they all want something. They want a piece of my father's land, or they want help with a peasant uprising, or they want me to marry their daughters. No one cares what I want. I want…

(He trails off and sighs again. The **NURSE** *enters.)*

NURSE. Daniel, here you are. The Royal Steward was ready to send out a search party.

DANIEL. Tell him not to worry. I just came out for some air.

NURSE. *You* tell him. I'm not going back in there – he was fit to be tied! He's taken care of all the royal affairs since your parents passed away, the least you could do is show up at a few of them.

DANIEL. I know. I'm sorry.

NURSE. There are a hundred beautiful girls in there, all waiting to dance with you.

DANIEL. I just don't feel like dancing today.

NURSE. *(looks closely at him)* Daniel, haven't I always taken good care of you?

DANIEL. Yes, you've been a wonderful Nurse.

NURSE. Well, you're twenty years old today. Far too old for a Nurse. I've stayed on because I promised your Mother.

DANIEL. I know.

NURSE. She always said that you were a dreamer. A star-gazer, she said. Always looking out there, never at what was right in front of your nose.

DANIEL. She used to say that to me, too.

NURSE. She thought it was because she spoiled you. And she did, you know. Spoiled you rotten. Let you go off for days at a time, never made you attend royal functions…

DANIEL. She was a good mother.

NURSE. I never said she wasn't. It was just hard for her to be strict with you. Poor dear, she didn't think she could ever have children.

DANIEL. I know.

NURSE. You were a miracle child, you were. Came just when your parents had given up hope.

DANIEL. I *know.*

NURSE. You think you know everything do you? Well, you listen to me. One year from today, you will inherit this entire kingdom – the lands, the palace, and the crown. So gaze out there as much as you want, Daniel. But never forget that you belong here. *(pause)* I'm going back to the party and, yes, I'll talk to the Steward. But I expect to see you in there shortly. Dancing. *(exits)*

DANIEL. I don't belong here. I never have.

SONG – I KNOW I'M NOT A PRINCE

I'VE ALWAYS FELT THAT I WAS OUT OF PLACE HERE
A NAGGING VOICE THAT WHISPERS IN MY MIND
IT TELLS ME OF A DIFFERENT HOME AND FAMILY
ANOTHER WORLD I SOMEHOW LEFT BEHIND

IT ISN'T THOUGH MY LIFE IS FULL OF HARDSHIPS
IT'S JUST AS ANY FAIRY TALE SHOULD BE
BUT IF I LIVED OUT THERE AMONG THE PEOPLE
I WONDER WHAT COULD HAVE BECOME OF ME

MY HEART ACHES WITH POSSIBILITIES
A PAIN I'VE FELT FROM YOUTH AND EVER SINCE
I CANNOT BEAR TO DWELL WITHIN THIS CASTLE
FOR DEEP INSIDE, I KNOW I'M NOT A PRINCE

IN MY DREAMS, I HEAR A WOMAN SINGING
OF STRENGTH AND LOVE AND CHOOSING WHAT IS
RIGHT
I CAN ALMOST SEE HER FACE WHEN I AWAKEN
BUT IT FADES TOO QUICKLY IN THE MORNING LIGHT

I CAN'T JUST WALK THIS PREDETERMINED PATHWAY
THE ROAD I TRAVEL WILL BE MINE TO TAKE
I'LL FIND THE HOME MY HEART HAS ALWAYS LONGED
FOR
AND HOW I LIVE WILL BE MY CHOICE TO MAKE

MY HEART ACHES WITH POSSIBILITIES
A PAIN I'VE FELT FROM YOUTH AND EVER SINCE
I CANNOT BEAR TO DWELL WITHIN THIS CASTLE
FOR DEEP INSIDE, I KNOW I'M NOT A PRINCE

LET ME RIDE THROUGH FRESHLY FALLEN SNOW
LET ME SWIM, LET ME CLIMB, LET ME SING
I'LL BE STRONG, LET ME FIND WHERE I BELONG
AND PLEASE DON'T ASK ME TO BE THE KING

MY HEART ACHES WITH POSSIBILITIES
A PAIN I'VE FELT FROM YOUTH AND EVER SINCE
I CANNOT BEAR TO DWELL WITHIN THIS CASTLE
FOR DEEP INSIDE, I KNOW I'M NOT A PRINCE
I'VE ALWAYS KNOWN THAT I AM NOT A PRINCE

I can't stay here. I can't stay and become king, not when I know there is something else out there for me. Tonight…I have to go tonight. *(He exits.)*

Scene Three

(Music continues under the scene change, as we reveal a tower in the middle of a forest. **RAPUNZEL** *and the* **WITCH** *are sitting together in front of a large cake. The* **WITCH** *is singing a Happy Birthday song.)*

WITCH. Make a wish and blow out your candles.

RAPUNZEL. My goodness! Twenty candles. I can hardly believe it.

WITCH. I know. My little girl is twenty years old. It seems like only yesterday I put you in this tower. Make a wish!

RAPUNZEL. Oh, Mother, it's the same wish I make every year. *(closes her eyes)* I wish that I will be safe and warm and taken care of for all of my days.

WITCH. What a wonderful wish. I'm sure it will come true. Now tell me what you've been doing today.

RAPUNZEL. Well, I sang a song, and I painted a picture. I unbraided my hair, but it got in the paint, so I braided it again. I guess that was all.

WITCH. So it was a good day, then.

RAPUNZEL. I suppose so. *(pause)* I saw a bird.

WITCH. *(cautiously)* What kind of a bird?

RAPUNZEL. A blue jay. It landed on the windowsill. Right there.

WITCH. You didn't touch it, did you?

RAPUNZEL. Oh course not, Mother! Honestly, do you think I *want* to sprout feathers and drop dead on the spot?!

WITCH. Exactly. Birds are dangerous, Rapunzel. Especially the blue ones.

RAPUNZEL. I know. It was pretty, though. And it sang such a beautiful song; it's strange that a creature so lovely can be so deadly.

WITCH. *(pause)* I think it's time for your lesson.

RAPUNZEL. Now? Oh, please, Mother, it's such a nice evening; do we have to have lessons now?

WITCH. Yes, we do. Now, go get the flash cards.

RAPUNZEL. Yes, Mother.

(She goes to the table and takes a bundle of oversized flash cards. They have pictures drawn on them.)

WITCH. Give them here. *(She takes them.)* Now, what is this? *(She holds up a picture of a daisy.)*

RAPUNZEL. *(By rote – she has had this lesson a million times.)*That is a daisy, also known as *bellis perennis.* The daisy is a perennial plant, it grows all year round, bearing flowers with white rays around a yellow disk.

WITCH. And what else do we know about the daisy?

RAPUNZEL. The petals are made of acid which, upon touching human skin, dissolves flesh and bone, causing death in under five minutes.

WITCH. Very good. *(Holds up a second flash card, with a picture of a rabbit.)* What is this?

RAPUNZEL. That is a rabbit, or *Oryctolagus cuniculus.* It is a burrowing mammal of the hare family, having soft fur and long ears.

WITCH. What else does a rabbit have?

RAPUNZEL. A rabbit has sharp, sharp teeth that will tear out a human throat in one large vicious bite.

WITCH. Excellent. You've been studying.

*(**RAPUNZEL** nods, pleased. The **WITCH** holds up another card with a picture of a man.)*

And this…?

RAPUNZEL. That is a man, or *homo sapien.* The most deadly of all woodland creatures. He will kidnap a woman from her comfortable home, force her to cook, clean and wait on him hand and foot.

RAPUNZEL. *(cont.)* Then, after many years, he will cast her aside for someone younger and more attractive, leaving her alone. *(pause)* To die.

WITCH. And what do you do if you see a man?

RAPUNZEL. Hide in my room, pretend I am not here and wait for him to go away.

WITCH. Good. The outside world is full of dangers, Rapunzel. Repeat that.

RAPUNZEL. The outside world is full of dangers.

WITCH. Your tower is the only place you will be safe. Repeat.

RAPUNZEL. My tower is the only place I will be safe.

*(She lays down with her head in the **WITCH**'s lap. The **WITCH** begins to sing.)*

(SONG – BE STRONG (REPRISE))

WITCH.
BE STRONG
YOU'RE NOT ALONE
I WILL BE HERE BESIDE YOU
FOLLOW MY LIGHT, CHOOSE WHAT IS RIGHT
MY CHILD
BE STRONG

RAPUNZEL. I love that song, Mother. Where did you learn it?

WITCH. I learned that song before you were born. From a foolish, foolish woman.

RAPUNZEL. Who was she?

WITCH. No one of importance.

RAPUNZEL. What became of her? Did she die? *(sympathetically)* She died, didn't she?

WITCH. She was a nasty woman. She stole something very special.

RAPUNZEL. How awful!

WITCH. But she was caught. And she was punished.

RAPUNZEL. Good. *(smiles)* Then it all worked out right in the end.

WITCH. Yes. It did. *(pause)* I must go now.

RAPUNZEL. Already?

WITCH. It's time.

RAPUNZEL. Please be careful, Mother. I worry so much when you're gone.

WITCH. There's no need to worry, my daughter. I have my magic to keep me safe.

RAPUNZEL. Your magic keeps me safe, too, doesn't it?

WITCH. Always. From roof to foundation, every inch of this tower is enchanted. As long as you stay inside, nothing can harm you.

RAPUNZEL. Thank you, Mother.

WITCH. Now, Rapunzel, let down your hair for me.

RAPUNZEL. Oh, of course. Here you are.

(She lets her hair down, and the **WITCH** *climbs to the ground.)*

I'll see you tomorrow!

WITCH. Sleep well, my little Rapunzel. *(She exits.)*

RAPUNZEL. Mmmmm. What a magnificent night. Look at all those stars. Each one watching over me. *(waves to the stars)* Hello, Mother! Good night! Don't worry about me! *(She begins to sing.)*
BE STRONG
YOU'RE NOT ALONE
I WILL BE HERE BESIDE YOU
FOLLOW MY LIGHT, DO WHAT IS RIGHT
MY CHILD
BE STRONG
BE STRONG

Scene Three

(The courtyard at night. **DANIEL** *is sneaking across the stage in semi-darkness, carrying a bag of clothing. He seems to hear* **RAPUNZEL**'s *voice echoing in the darkness. The* **NURSE** *is sitting on the bench, waiting for him.)*

NURSE. Beautiful night, isn't it?

DANIEL. *(startled)* Nurse! I thought you'd be asleep.

NURSE. I had a hunch that I should come down to the courtyard tonight. Always trust a woman's intuition.

DANIEL. I just had a bit of an upset stomach – probably from all the dancing. I thought I'd take a walk. The night air usually does me good.

NURSE. Just a walk? In your traveling shoes and with a bag of clothing?

DANIEL. *(silence for a moment as he looks at her)* All right, Nurse. I'm leaving. I'm running away tonight. Don't tell the Steward. Just pretend you never saw me. Please.

NURSE. I've seen this coming for a long time.

DANIEL. You have?

NURSE. I told your Mother she'd never be able to keep you here. She wouldn't believe it, but...

DANIEL. I'm sorry. They were wonderful parents – everyone has always been so good to me – but I'm just not a prince.

NURSE. You're right. You're not a prince.

DANIEL. What?

NURSE. Sit down, Daniel. It's time you knew the truth.

DANIEL. What truth? What do you mean?

NURSE. May your parents forgive me – I promised I would never tell.

DANIEL. Tell what?

NURSE. It was twenty years ago today. I was in the kitchen, fixing a cup of tea, when there was a terrific pounding at the door. I went to open it, and there was a little peasant girl, with a small bundle in her arms.

DANIEL. *(He is almost afraid to ask.)* What was in the bundle?

NURSE. A child. A baby boy. The girl told us that she had gone to fetch the water and, while she was at the well, a man ran up to her, gave her the baby and raced off. She didn't know what to do, so she brought the child to the palace.

DANIEL. What did you do?

NURSE. I took the baby. Your parents had been trying for years to have a child. This was the answer to their prayers.

DANIEL. But who was the man?

NURSE. We never knew. And we never told anyone. Your mother had stayed away from social occasions for months – no one suspected that you were not their child.

DANIEL. I wasn't their child. I could be anyone.

NURSE. No, Daniel. You're not just anyone. Your parents gave you their love and their devotion. You are their son.

DANIEL. But you see why I have to leave… I have to know who I am.

NURSE. No one can force you to be king, Daniel, least of all me. I'm just a nurse, and an old one at that. But I can tell you this – leave if you have to, find your answers. But you are a prince. And the day you realize that will be the day you return to us. Goodbye, Daniel. *(She exits.)*

DANIEL. Goodbye. Thank you!

I KNOW I'M NOT A PRINCE (REPRISE)

I WILL RIDE THROUGH FRESHLY FALLEN SNOW
I WILL SWIM, I WILL CLIMB, I'LL BE FREE
I'LL BE STRONG, I WILL FIND WHERE I BELONG
AND AT LAST, THE CHOICE IS UP TO ME

MY HEART IS FULL OF POSSIBILITIES
I'LL WALK THIS ROAD WHEREVER IT MIGHT LEAD
THROUGH FORESTS OVER MOUNTAINS TO THE OCEAN
UNTIL I HAVE THE ANSWERS THAT I NEED
ALL OF THE ANSWERS THAT I NEED

Scene Four

*(Back at the parent's cottage in the village. It's late at night. **FATHER** walks through the door, **MOTHER** is sitting, waiting for him.)*

MOTHER. It's late.

FATHER. I know. I went for a walk.

MOTHER. I see.

FATHER. I'll milk the cow in the morning.

MOTHER. Fine. I'll churn some butter tomorrow. *(pause)* I'm going to bed.

FATHER. It's a beautiful night. Would you like to come out with me?

MOTHER. No.

FATHER. Just down to the well. It might do you good.

MOTHER. I said no.

FATHER. Well, it does me good. Every year. Just to go there and sit. Say goodbye. Wish them a happy life.

MOTHER. *(stands up)* I'm not talking about this now.

FATHER. When are you ever talking about it? When, in the last twenty years have you talked about it? Our children are gone…

MOTHER. Stop…

FATHER. No. Not this time.

MOTHER. I can't do this.

FATHER. You have to do this.

MOTHER. No, I don't.

FATHER. I can't go on like this for another twenty years.

MOTHER. You don't understand.

FATHER. What don't I understand? They were my children, too.

MOTHER. It was your fault!

FATHER. *(pause)* What?

MOTHER. All of this. Everything that's happened. It was your fault. You never should have picked that lettuce.

FATHER. You asked me to! You begged me – nothing else would do, not fermented cucumbers, not frozen cow's milk with sugar – nothing! It had to be rapunzel!

MOTHER. And then you panicked, made that ridiculous bargain to give up our child.

FATHER. You agreed to it, as well.

MOTHER. And if you had just kept running! You could have saved our son – but you just left him with the first person you could find.

FATHER. I didn't know she would run off with him.

MOTHER. And we never found her.

FATHER. We searched for her. We searched for a year – we never found her. And we went through every neighboring forest looking for a tower.

MOTHER. They're gone. There's nothing we can do to bring them back, so why do we have to talk about them? It's easier to forget. Forget all of it. Milk the cow, clean the cottage, cook the meals. Awake in the morning and go to bed at night, and forget that for one moment, we were the happiest family in the world. *(Her voice breaks, but she fights it back.)*

SONG – THE MAGIC OF TEARS

FATHER.

HAVE YOU CRIED
FOR OUR CHILDREN?
HAVE YOU WEPT
SINCE THEY'VE BEEN GONE?
HAVE YOU LET THE FLOOD OF GRIEF
BREAK THROUGH THESE WALLS?
WHEN WAS THE LAST TIME
YOU SHED A TEAR?

MOTHER. I can't.

FATHER.

 THE MAGIC OF TEARS
 THE POWER OF HEALING
 A RUSH OF EMOTION
 FLOODS TO YOUR HEART
 THE MAGIC OF TEARS
 THAT STAGGERING FEELING
 THE SOUL AND THE BODY
 BREAKING APART
 THAT IS THE MAGIC OF TEARS

MOTHER.

 IT'S BEEN TOO LONG
 THAT ALL MY WORDS OF LOVE
 HAVE GONE UNSPOKEN
 I MUST BE STRONG
 TO KEEP MY BATTERED HEART
 FROM BEING BROKEN

FATHER.

 THE MAGIC OF TEARS
 COME LET ME HOLD YOU
 LET GO OF THE PAIN
 YOU'VE TRAPPED DEEP INSIDE
 TURNING BACK YEARS
 IT'S JUST AS I'VE TOLD YOU
 RELEASING THE ANGER
 YOU'VE NOTHING TO HIDE
 NOT FROM THE MAGIC OF TEARS

MOTHER.

 THEY SHOULD BE HERE
 I PROMISED I WOULD ALWAYS BE
 BESIDE THEM
 AND MY FEAR
 IS THERE'S NO PART OF ME THAT'S LEFT
 INSIDE THEM

BOTH.

>THE MAGIC OF TEARS
>EMBRACING THE GRIEVING
>WASHING THE WINDOWS
>INTO THE SOUL
>THERE'S MAGIC IN TEARS
>THE PAIN SLOWLY LEAVING
>HEALING THE HEART
>AND MAKING IT WHOLE
>THIS IS THE MAGIC OF TEARS
>THE MAGIC OF TEARS
>THE MAGIC OF TEARS

MOTHER. I'm sorry. I'm so sorry. All these years…

FATHER. …are over. We can begin again.

MOTHER. I love you.

FATHER. I love you. I always have.

MOTHER. Is it really a beautiful night?

FATHER. The most beautiful I've seen in twenty years.

MOTHER. Would you like to take a walk? We could go down to the well.

FATHER. Are you ready?

MOTHER. I am.

(She takes his hand – Blackout.)

Scene Five

(Back at the tower, two weeks later the **WITCH** *is brushing* **RAPUNZEL***'s hair.)*

RAPUNZEL. Ow. Ow! Ow! Stop. Stop stop stop stop stop!

WITCH. I can't stop. The brush is stuck in a knot back here. *(She pulls.)*

RAPUNZEL. Ouch! Mother, that hurt!

WITCH. I'm sorry, dear, but your hair is just so thick. It takes me hours to get the tangles out.

RAPUNZEL. Maybe it's time we cut it. It *is* awfully heavy.

WITCH. If we cut it, how would I get up here to your room? I need your hair to climb.

RAPUNZEL. I know, *(hopefully)* but perhaps if we built a ladder, or stairs…

WITCH. Rapunzel!

RAPUNZEL. *(chastened)* I'm sorry. I won't mention it again. Please, no lessons today.

WITCH. No lessons. I need to leave a bit earlier than usual.

RAPUNZEL. Oh no! But we were going to play cribbage. You promised!

WITCH. I know, but I have important things to tend to today. You can play solitaire.

RAPUNZEL. *(pouting)* I always play solitaire.

WITCH. Now, I don't want to hear any complaining. It takes hard work to keep you safe. You don't want anything to happen to your tower, do you?

RAPUNZEL. Of course not! Here. *(She lowers her hair.)* Climb on down; have a good afternoon.

WITCH. Thank you, my child. I'll be back tomorrow. *(She climbs down.)*

RAPUNZEL. Good-bye! Be careful!

(The **WITCH** *exits.* **RAPUNZEL** *picks up a deck of cards and begins to play, laying them out one at a time.)*

Two…five…Jack…butterfly. Butterfly eats Jack!

(She picks up the butterfly card and begins to attack the other cards with it, making chomping noises.)

RAPUNZEL. *(cont.)* Okay, next round. Seven…Ace…centipede.

(She throws the cards on the ground and begins stomping on them.)

Centipede crushes the ace with it's hundred pointy feet! Stomp! Stomp! Stomp! But butterfly eats centipede. Chomp! Chomp! Chomp!

(She rips up the centipede card and throws the pieces on the ground.)

Hmmm. Now what? Oooh! I'll paint a picture! A landscape!

(She picks up paper and paints and sets to work.)

A little brown…some black…now for the red… Perfect!

(She holds up a picture of an exploding volcano.)

This is what it looks like on that side of my tower. *(points to the side without a window)* I can hang it up, so it will be like another window. *(She does.)* Now what? I could do my exercises.

(She stretches her arms up above her head.)

Stretch…and touch my toes…

(She touches her toes, but the weight from her hair pulls her down and she falls flat on her stomach.)

Ow. I hate doing my exercises. Dumb hair.

(She sits, but she can't keep still and bounces up and down in the chair.)

RAPUNZEL. *(cont.)* I'm bored. Bo-o-o-o-ored. The trees are so green. It's a shame that the branches could twist around my neck and pull my head off – they're so pretty this time of year.

*(She begins to sing **BE STRONG** softly.)*

*(**DANIEL** enters, clothes a bit tattered, and sits down in the clearing. He doesn't see the tower.)*

DANIEL. I've been walking for two months. Two long months. Nothing but roads and pathways, one leading to another. It's wonderful! I've never felt so free in my life! And I'm getting close to something. I can just feel it.

SONG – BE STRONG (REPRISE 2)

RAPUNZEL.

BE STRONG
YOU'RE NOT ALONE
I WILL BE HERE BESIDE YOU
FOLLOW MY LIGHT, CHOOSE WHAT IS RIGHT
MY CHILD
BE STRONG

DANIEL. That voice. It's the voice from my dream. It's the song – the same song. Where is it coming from?

*(He sees **RAPUNZEL** in her tower.)*

Hello? Hello up there!

RAPUNZEL. *(sees **DANIEL** and lets out a bloodcurdling scream)*

DANIEL. No! Wait! I won't hurt you!

RAPUNZEL. *(continues to scream)*

DANIEL. Stop! Please! It's all right!

RAPUNZEL. You're a man! *(begins to recite to try and remain calm)* Homo sapien. The most deadly of all the woodland creatures. *(in a panic)* I won't cook and clean and wait on you hand and foot! Go away!

DANIEL. Wait a minute! I just want to talk to you.

RAPUNZEL. No you don't! You want me to be your slave and then turn me out and leave me to die!

DANIEL. Whoa! I have no idea what you're talking about.

RAPUNZEL. Mother told me all about you. All about men. I...I have a flash card!

DANIEL. OK, let's just take a breath and start from the beginning. Your mother told you what?

RAPUNZEL. About the world. How dangerous it is. About how the grass grows up around your feet and makes you stuck in one spot until you starve, and how acorns look small but they weigh 500 pounds and will crush your head if they land on you, and how baby deer shoot poisonous arrows out of their big round eyes....

(DANIEL *begins to laugh.*)

What? Why are you laughing?

DANIEL. I'm sorry...I just...poisonous arrows? *(He continues to laugh.)*

RAPUNZEL. Stop laughing at me!

DANIEL. All right. I'll stop. *(He takes a big breath and controls himself.)* See? I'm not laughing anymore.

RAPUNZEL. I suppose you're going to try and kidnap me now. Well, I should warn you that you can't touch this tower. It's completely enchanted.

DANIEL. The tower's enchanted?

RAPUNZEL. Every inch of it. If you even lay one finger on it, you'll disappear in a big puff of smoke.

(DANIEL *walks up to the tower, holds out his index finger and deliberately touches the tower.)*

DANIEL. Hmm. Still here. *(He touches himself.)* I don't feel like a puff of smoke.

RAPUNZEL. How did you do that?

DANIEL. I guess I must be magic. Come down here; I want to talk to you.

RAPUNZEL. I can't come down.

DANIEL. Well, then I'll come up there. Where's the door?

RAPUNZEL. There is no door.

DANIEL. What do you mean, there's no door? There has to be a door. How do you get out?

RAPUNZEL. I don't.

DANIEL. You don't?

RAPUNZEL. I've never been out. It's far too dangerous.

DANIEL. Because of the acorns.

RAPUNZEL. Acorns are just the beginning. Mother says my tower is the only place I will be safe. And she knows everything. She's magic, too.

DANIEL. Really? Where is your mother, now?

RAPUNZEL. She's gone for the day. She usually comes to see me in the afternoons, but she left early today. She has awfully important things to do.

DANIEL. How does she get up there?

RAPUNZEL. She climbs my hair. See? *(She lets her hair fall down the outside of the tower.)*

DANIEL. Wow! That's a lot of hair! Do you think I could climb it?

RAPUNZEL. Well…I'm not supposed to ever talk to anyone. Or anything. But I suppose if you're magic, too, it might be all right. You can protect me, like Mother does. OK. Go ahead and climb up.

(He begins to climb.)

Ow! You're heavier than Mother. Don't pull so hard!

(He reaches the top and climbs in her window. She rubs her head.)

I hope you bounce, cause you're not climbing back down.

DANIEL. I wanted to ask you about the song you were singing.

RAPUNZEL. What about it?

DANIEL. How did you?…Who?…Where did you learn it?

RAPUNZEL. My mother taught it to me.

DANIEL. The mother with the magic and the…the flash cards?

RAPUNZEL. Well, she didn't make it up or anything. She learned it from some mean lady who stole something and died. Why do you want to know?

DANIEL. It's nothing…it's just that…I've heard that song. In my dreams. A woman sings it to me. I can't quite make out her face, but I know she's beautiful. And I feel safe and warm and…

TOGETHER. Loved. *(They look at each other.)*

RAPUNZEL. I have that same dream sometimes. That's odd, isn't it? Mother told me it's a remembering dream. About when she used to sing to me when I was a baby. But why would you be remembering my mother?

DANIEL. *(getting excited)* What does your mother look like?

RAPUNZEL. Oh, I drew a picture of her. It's here some-where.

(She goes through the stack of papers on the table.)

She always said it was an excellent likeness.

(She holds up a drawing of the Witch, in all her hideousness.)

Here it is. Is this the woman in your dreams?

DANIEL. *(both disappointed and relieved)* I don't think so.

RAPUNZEL. Now that I think about it, the voice in my dream isn't anything like Mother's. *(She scrunches her eyes shut.)* And the woman in my dream is tall, and she has blonde hair. And when the light is behind her, it looks like a halo.

DANIEL. *(scrunches up his eyes, too)* And she's wearing a blue dress with white trim…

RAPUNZEL. She's in a cottage…

DANIEL. …with a little window

RAPUNZEL. And there's a man there, too…

DANIEL. He's tall…

TOGETHER. …and they're laughing.

(They open their eyes and stare at each other.)

TOGETHER. Who *are* you? Who are *you?*

RAPUNZEL. I don't understand. I don't understand.

DANIEL. All right, stay calm. My name is Daniel. Until a few weeks ago, I was a prince. Then I found out that my parents weren't really my parents. I was given to them by a man – I think he must have been my father, but no one knows who he was. I've been looking for him, and for my mother ever since. Now…who are you?

RAPUNZEL. My name is Rapunzel. I've lived in this tower for as long as I can remember. My Mother brings me food and takes care of me and teaches me everything I need to know.

DANIEL. You don't remember anything before you came to this tower?

RAPUNZEL. No, I've been here my whole life.

DANIEL. How old are you?

RAPUNZEL. I'm twenty. I just had my birthday two weeks ago. Mother baked a cake. Without eggs. If eggs aren't cooked all the way, they give you food poisoning and you die.

DANIEL. They don't give you food poison…oh…OK – But wait a minute! My twentieth birthday was two weeks ago!

RAPUNZEL. What does that mean?

DANIEL. I don't know, Rapunzel. But I'm going to find out. Let your hair down, I'm going to find your Mother.

RAPUNZEL. Be careful! She's magic. And she really, really doesn't like men.

DANIEL. She won't hurt me.

RAPUNZEL. Why? What are you going to do? You're not going to hurt her, are you?

DANIEL. I just want answers. She seems like the best place to start.

RAPUNZEL. You'll come back soon?

DANIEL. I'll come back soon.

(blackout)

Scene Six

(Another part of the wood. The **WITCH** *is raking a vegetable patch and talking to herself.)*

WITCH. Lettuce and tomatoes and cabbages and peas. The ground here is wrong for peppers, but come summertime I should have a nice batch of corn. Now if I could just figure out a way to keep the squirrels away. *(She chuckles.)* Maybe I should just tell them that corn will pop in their stomachs and they'll explode.

DANIEL. *(offstage)* Hello! Is anyone out here?

WITCH. No one ever comes this deep into the forest. Someone lost, no doubt. I'll send him on his way. Far away. *(calls out, in an innocent old lady voice)* Hello? Is there someone there?

DANIEL. *(entering)* Hello? *(He sees the* **WITCH.***)* Oh! Perhaps you can help me.

WITCH. You must be lost, poor thing. The path is just through the clearing there – follow that till it forks, make a left, a right, another left, and you'll be home before you know it. Off you go!

DANIEL. I'm afraid you don't understand. I'm not lost.

WITCH. You're not?

DANIEL. No. I'm looking for someone.

WITCH. Well, no one would be foolish enough to live out here. You must be looking in the wrong forest.

DANIEL. *(takes a risk)* I'm looking for Rapunzel's mother.

WITCH. How do you know that name?

DANIEL. Are you her mother?

WITCH. *(intimidating)* How do you know about Rapunzel?

DANIEL. OK, um…Hello.

(He holds out his hand in his most polite and princely fashion.)

DANIEL. *(cont.)* It is so nice to make your acquaintance. My name is Daniel, and I was wondering if I could ask you a couple of questions…

(She doesn't take his hand; he withdraws it.)

OK. *(He tries a different tactic.)* I found her tower back there, and we chatted a bit – there were a few details that I thought you might be able to help me with…

WITCH. It's you!

DANIEL. Who?

WITCH. You can't have her back.

DANIEL. Excuse me?

WITCH. I know who you are – you've come to try and get her back. And where is her mother? Is she here, too?

DANIEL. Her mother?

WITCH. Don't act the fool! I won't let you take her.

DANIEL. I'm afraid I still don't understand. You're not Rapunzel's mother?

WITCH. It was a fair trade! You know it was a fair trade. You took my lettuce, I took your child!

DANIEL. My child? What lettuce?

WITCH. Is she afraid to face me? I wouldn't be surprised – I beat her the last time. And you! You weren't even there. You didn't even bother to protect your wife and daughter. You just ran away.

DANIEL. I don't know what you're talking about! My name is Daniel. I don't have a wife or a daughter. I'm only twenty years old.

WITCH. *(stares at him)* Twenty years old. A twin. No wonder he ran away – he left to save the boy. Well, there is no saving you this time.

(She picks up the rake and swings it at him.)

DANIEL. Hey!

WITCH. Did you think it would be that simple? *(She lands a blow.)*

DANIEL. Ow! Stop that!

WITCH. She won't ever leave her tower.

(She swings again, he ducks.)

WITCH. *(cont.)* She doesn't want to leave!

(She swings again, he rolls out of the way.)

DANIEL. She's too afraid to leave, you mean. You've filled her head with stories and lies!

(She hits him in the back and he falls down, rolling over onto his back – during the following exchange, she slams the rake in the ground on either side of his head, he rolls out of the way each time.)

WITCH. She'll never go with you! She's safe there. And you're dead!

(She brings the rake down, but he grabs it.)

DANIEL. I wouldn't be so sure of that.

(He throws her backward and she falls on the ground.)

My turn,

(He hits her with the rake and knocks her unconscious. He goes to her.)

She's still alive. I have to get Rapunzel out of there before she wakes up.

(He runs off. Blackout.)

Scene Seven

(The tower. **RAPUNZEL** *is waiting nervously.* **DANIEL** *comes running up.)*

DANIEL. Rapunzel! Rapunzel! Let down your hair!

RAPUNZEL. Daniel? Is that you? Where's Mother?

DANIEL. She's not your mother.

RAPUNZEL. What?

DANIEL. That woman is not your mother. Your mother is my mother. I don't have time to explain – let me up!

RAPUNZEL. *(lets down her hair. As he climbs:)* I don't understand what you're saying. Whose Mother? Daniel, tell me what you're talking about!

DANIEL. The woman that you thought was your mother isn't really your mother. She stole you – there was something about lettuce, I didn't understand that part, but your mother tried to protect you. And your father tried to protect me.

RAPUNZEL. You?

DANIEL. I'm your brother.

RAPUNZEL. What?

DANIEL. I'm your brother. We're twins!

RAPUNZEL. This doesn't make any sense.

DANIEL. It will; I promise it will, but we have to leave now.

RAPUNZEL. But where is Mother?

DANIEL. There was a fight – she's really strong for an old lady – and I hit her with a rake.

RAPUNZEL. You hit Mother?

DANIEL. Listen to me. She isn't your mother. She stole you from our parents when you were just a baby.

RAPUNZEL. I don't think she would do that – she told me stealing is wrong.

DANIEL. That might be the only thing she told you that's actually true.

RAPUNZEL. What?

DANIEL. Rapunzel, you need to believe me. The woman you thought was your mother is a very bad person. She's unconscious right now, but she could wake up any time. We have to get out of here before she gets back!

RAPUNZEL. I can't go.

DANIEL. You have to believe me!

RAPUNZEL. Oh, I believe you – I guess. I mean, we have the same dream and everything, so it makes sense. But I can't leave the tower.

DANIEL. Yes, you can.

RAPUNZEL. I can't. I really, really can't.

SONG – I CAN'T GO

> I'D REALLY LIKE TO GO WITH YOU
> I REALLY TRULY WOULD
> AFTER HEARING WHAT YOU'VE TOLD ME
> I KNOW I PROB'LY SHOULD
> BUT I CAN'T GO

DANIEL. Why?

RAPUNZEL.

> I WILL GLADLY TELL YOU WHY
> THE AIR OUTSIDE IS TOXIC IF I BREATHE IT I WILL DIE!

DANIEL. You won't die.

RAPUNZEL. Yes, I will.

> MOTHER PUT A FORCEFIELD ROUND MY TOWER

DANIEL. A forcefield?

RAPUNZEL.

> A BUBBLE THAT PROTECTS ME FROM THE AIR

DANIEL. I don't see any bubble.

RAPUNZEL.

> IT'S INVISIBLE BUT STILL IT HAS GREAT POWER

DANIEL. This is ridiculous!

RAPUNZEL.

>IT SHIELDS ME FROM THE NOXIOUS FUMES OUT
>THERE.

DANIEL. OK, Rapunzel, listen to me.

>I KNOW THAT YOU ARE FRIGHTENED
>BUT THERE'S NOTHING THERE TO FEAR
>IT'S ONLY AIR, THE SAME OUT THERE
>AS WHAT YOU BREATHE IN HERE

RAPUNZEL. Really?

DANIEL. Yes. Now can we get out of this tower?

RAPUNZEL.

>I'D REALLY LIKE TO GO WITH YOU
>I REALLY TRULY WOULD
>NOW I KNOW THE AIR'S NOT POISONED
>SO I KNOW I PROB'LY SHOULD
>BUT I CAN'T LEAVE

DANIEL. Why?

RAPUNZEL.

>CAN'T LEAVE THIS TOWER WHERE I'VE DWELT
>WATER COMES DOWN FROM THE SKY AND IF IT
>TOUCHES ME I'LL MELT

DANIEL. You won't melt.

RAPUNZEL. Yes I will!

>MOTHER BUILT A MAGICAL RAIN BARREL

DANIEL. There's no magic.

RAPUNZEL.

>IT COLLECTS THE WATER, THEN IT MAKES IT CLEAN

DANIEL. But Rapunzel…

RAPUNZEL.

>SO WHEN I BATHE OR WASH OUT MY APPAREL

DANIEL. Wait a minute…

RAPUNZEL.

>MY SKIN WON'T PEEL AWAY AND TURN ALL GREEN

DANIEL. Stop!
> I'M SORRY IF I'M RUSHING
> YOU NEED TO TAKE THINGS SLOW
> BUT FEEL NO PAIN, FOR WHEN THERE'S RAIN
> IT HELPS TO MAKE THINGS GROW

RAPUNZEL. It won't make me melt?

DANIEL. No. Now get your coat and come on!

RAPUNZEL.
> I'D REALLY LIKE TO GO WITH YOU
> I REALLY TRULY WOULD
> AND NOW I'M NOT AFRAID OF WATER
> SO I KNOW I PROB'LY SHOULD
> BUT I CAN'T GO

DANIEL. Why?

RAPUNZEL.
> YOU SEE MY SITUATION'S DIRE
> THE GROUND OUTSIDE IS CRUMBLING IF I TOUCH IT
> I'LL EXPIRE!

DANIEL. You won't expire!

RAPUNZEL. Yes, I will!
> MOTHER MADE MY HOME WITHOUT A STAIRCASE

DANIEL. She's not your mother.

RAPUNZEL.
> BECAUSE THE EARTH IS WILD AND UNBOUND

DANIEL. It's just dirt.

RAPUNZEL.
> IF I WERE TO EVER LEAVE THIS RARE PLACE

DANIEL. Do you even own a coat?

RAPUNZEL.
> I'D BE SWALLOWED UP AND NEVER FOUND!

DANIEL. The earth won't swallow you up.
> PLEASE TRUST ME SISTER
> THE GROUND IS SOLID STONE
> HAVE FAITH SOMEHOW, WE'RE GOING NOW
> I WILL NOT LEAVE ALONE.

RAPUNZEL.

> I'D REALLY LIKE TO COME WITH YOU
> I REALLY TRULY WOULD
> BUT AFTER ALL YOU'VE TOLD ME
> I DON'T BELIEVE I SHOULD

RAPUNZEL.	**DANIEL.**
I'M SO VERY FRIGHTENED	PLEASE COME WITH ME
IF IT'S TRUE WHAT YOU HAVE	
SAID	
THEN MY MOTHER IS A LIAR	THE WORLD IS BIG AND WIDE
AND I MIGHT AS WELL BE DEAD	
I CANNOT LEAVE MY TOWER	HAVE FAITH SOMEHOW,
	WE'RE GOING NOW
IT'S THE ONLY HOME I'VE	
KNOWN	
HOW CAN I BE WITH PEOPLE	DON'T HIDE IN FEAR INSIDE
WHEN I'VE ALWAYS LIVED	
ALONE?	

DANIEL.

> TAKE MY HAND, MY SISTER

RAPUNZEL.

> NEVER LET ME GO

DANIEL.

> COME WITH ME AND YOU'LL BE FREE
> OUT IN THE WORLD BELOW

TOGETHER.

> BE STRONG
> BE STRONG
> BE STRONG
> WE'RE NOT ALONE

RAPUNZEL. I'll go.

DANIEL. Good! We have to leave right now. There's no telling when she'll get here.

RAPUNZEL. Are you sure she's still alive?

DANIEL. Positive. I didn't hit her that hard – just enough to knock her out. Do you have everything you need?

RAPUNZEL. I suppose there's no way to take my paints is there?

DANIEL. We'll get you new paints. Come on.

RAPUNZEL. Wait a minute! How are we both going to get down?

DANIEL. I have an idea, but you might not like it.

RAPUNZEL. What is it?

DANIEL. *(breaking it to her gently)* We have to cut your hair.

RAPUNZEL. Really?

DANIEL. I know it's going to be hard for you; I'm sure you're very attached to it – well, of course you're attached to it, but –

RAPUNZEL. Are you joking? Stay right there, I'll get the scissors!

DANIEL. You don't mind?

RAPUNZEL. Mind? I hate this hair. It weighs a ton and takes forever to brush. Here! *(She hands him scissors.)* Get rid of it!

DANIEL. Here goes… *(He cuts off her hair.)* Are you okay?

RAPUNZEL. I feel light as a feather.

DANIEL. Let's tie it to the table leg. That should support us going down. *(They tie it.)* Ready?

RAPUNZEL. Ready.

> *(They climb down the hair to the ground – as they climb…)*

> The ground *will* hold me up…The air *won't* be toxic…The ants *can't* dig a five foot hole, bury me up to my neck and nibble out my eyeballs…

DANIEL. No, they really can't.

RAPUNZEL. *(putting a foot on the ground)* I did it. I'm standing on the ground. *(She jumps up and down tentatively.)* I'm outside my tower. *(starting to hyperventilate)* I'm outside my tower.

DANIEL. You're doing fine. Now, we're going to have to run. Ready…set…

*(The **WITCH** steps out in front of them.)*

WITCH. Go.

(They gasp.)

DANIEL. Run, Rapunzel!

*(They try to run, but the **WITCH** throws a net over both of them.)*

RAPUNZEL. Daniel, help! I'm stuck!

DANIEL. I'm just as stuck as you are. *(to **WITCH**)* Let us go!

WITCH. You hit me with a rake. I'm not exactly feeling charitable.

DANIEL. You tried to kill me!

RAPUNZEL. Mother, please!

WITCH. I'm not your Mother. I'm sure your twin here has filled you in on all the details.

DANIEL. Yes, I did. You're a kidnapper and you destroyed our family!

WITCH. Wrong! It's so easy to blame me, isn't it? Well, that's not the whole story. *I* am the injured party here.

RAPUNZEL. I don't understand.

WITCH. Well try.

SONG - WITCH'S SONG

*(During this song, **DANIEL** and **RAPUNZEL** figure out a way to loosen themselves from the net, being careful that the **WITCH** doesn't notice what they're doing)*

WHEN I WAS A CHILD
I DIDN'T PLAY WITH OTHER GIRLS
I HUNG BACK FAR TOO SHY TO MAKE MY NAME KNOWN
SO I WATCHED AND I ENVIED

WITCH. *(cont.)*

THEIR BLONDE AND BOUNCY CURLS
AS I SPENT EVERY LONELY DAY ALONE

I'D PRETEND I DIDN'T CARE
WHAT A PITIFUL CHARADE
WITH MY BOOKS AND MY CAST-OFF, PATCHED-UP
BLOUSES
WHEN I LONGED FOR FINE JEWELRY
AND A BALL GOWN NEWLY MADE
TO SIP TEA IN THE FINEST VILLAGE HOUSES

BUT I KNEW SOMEDAY I WOULD PROVE THAT I WAS
WORTHY
THEY WOULD SEE WHAT THEY HAD PUSHED ASIDE FOR
YEARS
AT LAST I'D BE WORSHIPPED, PAINTED, LOVED,
RESPECTED
SILLY VILLAGE GIRLS WOULD CHOKE ON BITTER
TEARS.
LATE ONE NIGHT
I WAS READING BY MY FLAME
DUSTY MANUSCRIPTS THAT LAY BEHIND THE STABLE
INSIDE THOSE RATTED PAGES
WAS THE SECRET TO MY FAME
AND I SPREAD THEM OUT ACROSS THE KITCHEN TABLE

A SEED ONE SEED
JUST ONE LITTLE TINY SPECK
CONTAINED MY FUTURE AS A GENUIS UNCONTESTED
IT WAS JUST ONE SEED
BUT I FIGURED WHAT THE HECK
AND I CHECKED THE BOOK TO SEE WHAT IT
SUGGESTED

AND I KNEW AT ONCE THAT OPPORTUNITY HAD
KNOCKED
WITH THE PROMISE OF A PRODUCE RARE AND BOLD
NOT AN ORDINARY LETTUCE, GREEN AND DESPERATELY
DULL
BUT RAPUNZEL – MORE VALUABLE THAN GOLD

WITCH. *(cont.)*

RAPUNZEL IS SCARCE
FOR AS I QUICKLY LEARNED
IT TAKES TWENTY YEARS TO RIPEN IN THE GROUND
BUT PEOPLE PAY A BUNDLE
AND IT'S MONEY RIGHTLY EARNED
IF AN INTERESTED BUYER CAN BE FOUND

I TOILED FOR DECADES
AS THE GIRLS AROUND ME MARRIED
HAVING CHILDREN OF THEIR OWN WHO CAME TO JEER
BUT I KEPT TO MY TASK
TO THIS BURDEN THAT I CARRIED
AS I WATCHED MY FORTUNES DRAWING EVER NEAR

AND THEN YOUR CHARMING PARENTS MOVED TO
TOWN
AND ALL OF MY AMBITIONS TUMBLED DOWN

THE QUEEN UP ON THE HILL
MADE AN OFFER HUGE AND WILD
SHE AGREED TO PAY A THOUSAND POUNDS OF GOLD
SHE HEARD RAPUNZEL LETTUCE
COULD HELP HER HAVE A CHILD
SHE'D ARRIVE AT DAWN TO SEE THAT IT WAS SOLD
IT WAS LATE, IT WAS DARK
YOUR MOTHER HAD A CRAVING
FOR A BIT OF LEAFY LETTUCE WITH HER MEAT
YOUR FATHER CLIMBED THE WALL
TO THE YARD WHERE I'D BEEN SLAVING
AND HE PICKED HIS WIFE A TASTY LITTLE TREAT

AND I KNEW THAT DAY THAT ALL MY LIFE WAS WASTED
I WOULD NEVER HAVE THE FAME FOR WHICH I
YEARNED
SO I MAKE YOUR DAD A DEAL, WHICH HE GRACIOUSLY
ACCEPTED
AND I TOOK THE DAUGHTER I FELT I HAD EARNED
I AM STRONG! WAS THE LESSON THEY HAD LEARNED
MY SOUL WAS ON FIRE
AND IT BURNED!

WITCH. *(cont.)* So try, just try to escape. *(to* **DANIEL***)* Soon, you'll be dead *(to* **RAPUNZEL***)* and you'll be right back in your tower where you belong.

RAPUNZEL. Wait. There's something I need to know.

WITCH. And what is that?

RAPUNZEL. *(emerging from the net)* What kind of a person spends her entire life growing one plant, just because a bunch of bratty little girls were mean to her? Twenty years for one little batch of whatever that lettuce was called –

DANIEL. *(telling her the name of the lettuce)* Rapunzel.

RAPUNZEL. Not now, Daniel, I'm talking. You could have been anything, done whatever you wanted, and you threw it all away because you were so bitter and angry.

WITCH. But…wait…that's not how it happened…your parents ruined my life…

RAPUNZEL. No they didn't. They took your lettuce, yes, but your life was already ruined.

WITCH. All of those girls made fun of me – I would make them see that I was stronger than they were.

DANIEL. You're not strong. Revenge isn't strong. Strength is admitting your mistakes and forgiving others for theirs.

RAPUNZEL & DANIEL. Strength is choosing what's right.

DANIEL. Let's go, Rapunzel.

WITCH. You still don't get it, do you? I'll never let you go! *(She pulls a knife out of her dress and swings it at* **DANIEL***.)*

RAPUNZEL. Daniel, look out!

WITCH. *(as she chases* **DANIEL** *toward the tower)* She is mine! I raised her from a seed, watered her, watched her grow!

DANIEL. *(climbs the hair up to the tower)* She isn't your lettuce! She is a girl! You can't own her!

RAPUNZEL. Daniel, be careful!

WITCH. *(climbing up after him)* I should have had fame and fortune! I had to settle for a child.

DANIEL. *(in the tower)* She's not your child. You're supposed to love children– not lock them in towers and frighten them.

WITCH. I raised her! That makes her my daughter.

RAPUNZEL. Daniel!

DANIEL. Fine – she's your daughter. But you're forgetting something.

(grabbing the **WITCH** *as she tries to pull herself up into the window)*

She's my sister!

(He pushes the **WITCH** *out the window, but she grabs onto him at the last moment and they both fall to the ground, into a large thorn bush.* **RAPUNZEL** *screams. The* **WITCH** *is killed, and* **DANIEL***'s eyes are blinded.)*

RAPUNZEL. Daniel? Daniel!

DANIEL. *(getting up)* Rapunzel? Rapunzel, I can't see you. Where are you?

RAPUNZEL. I'm here.

DANIEL. The Witch? Where is she?

RAPUNZEL. I think she's dead. Daniel, your eyes! What happened to your eyes?

DANIEL. The thorns. In the bush – I fell into the thorns. Rapunzel, I can't see.

RAPUNZEL. Oh, Daniel! *(She embraces him.)* What will we do?

DANIEL. We have to get out of this forest. If we can just get back to the palace…but I can't tell which way…I can't guide us…

RAPUNZEL. I'll guide the way.

DANIEL. Are you sure? You've never left your tower. It'll be like the blind leading the blind.

RAPUNZEL. *(jittery, but brave)* I can do it. I can be brave. I'll be strong. We just need to stay away from thorn bushes.

(She takes his hand and they begin to walk.)

And moss.

DANIEL. Why moss?

RAPUNZEL. It squirts poison.

DANIEL. Rapunzel…

RAPUNZEL. Oh! *(She pulls on his arm.)* Careful!

DANIEL. What?!

RAPUNZEL. Acorns.

DANIEL. Right. Acorns.

(They exit. Blackout)

Scene Eight

(A clearing in another part of the woods. **MOTHER** *and* **FATHER** *are sitting on a log.)*

FATHER. How do you feel today?

MOTHER. Sad. A little wistful. But it's good to feel something.

FATHER. Do you want to talk about it?

MOTHER. *(smiles)* I do. I was just thinking about where they are right now – what they look like, what they're doing. Sometimes, when I walk home from market, I see the young peasant men in the fields and I wonder if one of them is my son.

FATHER. I was thinking – it might be time to look again. Perhaps we could ask the palace for help. The Prince has one more year before he becomes king – maybe he has time to offer some assistance.

MOTHER. I hardly think the royal family is going to take an interest in our affairs, but I suppose there's no harm in trying. After all, it isn't as though we'll be clapped in jail for lettuce theft after all these years.

FATHER. They could be anywhere. A thousand miles away and a thousand miles apart.

MOTHER. I don't know. There is a part of me that feels as though they're quite close.

(There is a commotion offstage, and **RAPUNZEL** *enters, leading* **DANIEL.** *)*

RAPUNZEL. OK, there's a patch of grass to your left – step over it. Step over it! And don't walk through that puddle!

MOTHER. *(sees that* **DANIEL** *is injured)* My goodness! What happened?

RAPUNZEL. He fell into a thorn bush. He can't see anything and I'm trying to get him back to the palace.

FATHER. The palace? Aren't you the Prince?

DANIEL. Yes, I am. Do I know you?

MOTHER. Of course not, we're just farmers. But please, sit. Let us help you.

(She guides him to the log and begins dabbing at his eyes with a handkerchief.)

DANIEL. You are very kind. Thank you. I'm Daniel, and this is my sister.

FATHER. I didn't realize there was a princess.

RAPUNZEL. Oh, I'm not a princess.

DANIEL. It's rather a long story.

RAPUNZEL. I'm Rapunzel.

(MOTHER *and* **FATHER** *freeze.)*

MOTHER. What did you say?

DANIEL. It's a strange name, I know. She was named after a rare variety of lettuce.

RAPUNZEL. *(finally gets it)* Oh!

MOTHER & FATHER. Lettuce?!

RAPUNZEL. You see, I was raised in a tower by a witch who named me after some lettuce that she grew that my real parents stole so she kidnapped me twenty years ago to take her revenge and this is my twin brother who found me by accident and helped me escape, but now he's blind and I don't know how to get back to the castle and do you think you could help us?

(MOTHER *and* **FATHER** *stare at her.)*

What?

(MOTHER *begins to cry,* **FATHER** *holds onto her.)*

RAPUNZEL. Oh dear, you're crying. Please don't cry –

DANIEL. Are you all right?

MOTHER. We found you.

FATHER. We found them.

MOTHER. And they're together. *(She goes to* **RAPUNZEL.***)* You're so beautiful. You're just as I pictured you.

RAPUNZEL. Who are you?

MOTHER. *(She goes to* **DANIEL.***)* And Daniel. I watched you grow up – I didn't miss it. Oh, there are so many things I want to tell you – tell both of you. I've missed you so much!

DANIEL. Are you…. are you…Mother?

RAPUNZEL. With the blue dress…and the song…? *(She runs to her.)* Mother!

DANIEL. Father?

FATHER. I'm here, Daniel. I'm here.

(They all embrace.)

MOTHER. My children. I have my children.

DANIEL. But I can't see you. I can't see.

RAPUNZEL. She's beautiful, Daniel. And Father is so handsome.

(She turns to **FATHER** *and they embrace, leaving* **MOTHER** *and* **DANIEL.***)*

MOTHER. My children. I have waited for twenty years to tell you how much I love you.

DANIEL. Mother, you're crying. Please don't cry. We found each other.

MOTHER. Don't be afraid to cry, Daniel. There's magic in tears.

(She reaches up and wipes her tears away, then touches **DANIEL***'s eyes.)*

SONG - THE MAGIC OF TEARS (REPRISE)

MOTHER.
THE MAGIC OF TEARS
THE JOY AND THE SORROW
EMBRACING EMOTIONS
LEARNING TO FEEL

MOTHER. *(cont.)*
THE MAGIC OF TEARS
DON'T WAIT FOR TOMORROW
LOVING AND GRIEVING
BEGINNING TO HEAL
THIS IS THE MAGIC OF TEARS
THE MAGIC OF TEARS
THE MAGIC OF –

DANIEL. *(blinks his eyes – his sight is restored)* Mother?

(He reaches for her, then turns to **FATHER** *and* **RAPUNZEL.***)*

Father? I can see you. I can see you!

RAPUNZEL. It's magic! It's really magic!

MOTHER. Daniel? You can see?

DANIEL. I can see you; I can see Father – I can see every-thing!

(He runs to **RAPUNZEL,** *picks her up and twirls her around.)*

I can see!

RAPUNZEL. Careful!

(He puts her down, she touches her face.)

Did my nose fall off?

DANIEL. No, your nose didn't fall off.

FATHER. Why would her nose have fallen off?

DANIEL. Don't ask. *(He laughs.)* What a beautiful world. Has it always been this beautiful?

MOTHER. It doesn't matter. I have my children.

(She sits with them on the log.)

FATHER. There's something I don't understand. How did you get to be the prince?

MOTHER. That's right. You gave him to a peasant girl.

DANIEL. She took me to the palace. The king and queen couldn't have children, so they raised me as their own.

MOTHER. All this time – you were right there at the top of the hill. *(to* **RAPUNZEL***)* And you, at the top of a tower. You poor thing.

RAPUNZEL. Oh, I didn't mind it so much. The world is awfully big. And very scary.

MOTHER. You have us, now. We won't let anything harm you. Never again.

FATHER. So what do we do now?

RAPUNZEL. What do you mean?

FATHER. Well, I don't suppose you want to come home with us, do you?

MOTHER. It's a small cottage but it's quite nice, with a vegetable garden in front and rabbits in the back.

RAPUNZEL. You keep rabbits? *(hyperventilating)* As pets?

DANIEL. I have a better idea.

RAPUNZEL. Oh, thank goodness.

DANIEL. Come live in the palace with me.

FATHER. The palace?

MOTHER. Oh, we couldn't!

DANIEL. Yes, you can. I'm seeing things very clearly right now – more clearly than I ever have before. My parents – the king and queen, I mean – they loved me very much, and they raised me to be the king. Now I realize that they were right – I should be the king. But I want to rule with you – all of you – by my side. Say you'll come with me…

FATHER. I would be honored, Your Majesty.

(They laugh.)

MOTHER. The palace! Are you sure?

DANIEL. I'm sure. How about you, Rapunzel?

RAPUNZEL. Are there rabbits at the palace?

DANIEL. No, but there are excellent teachers – we'll get you started on lessons right away. *Real* lessons.

RAPUNZEL. I'll go!

MOTHER. We'll all go. As a family.

DANIEL. A family…

SONG - I KNOW I'M NOT A PRINCE (REPRISE 2)

LET ME RIDE THROUGH FRESHLY FALLEN SNOW
LET ME SWIM LET ME CLIMB LET ME SING
I'LL BE STRONG; I HAVE FOUND WHERE I BELONG
AT LAST, I CHOOSE TO BE THE KING

MY HEART IS FULL OF POSSIBILITIES
I'LL WALK THIS ROAD WHEREVER IT MAY LEAD
THROUGH FORESTS, OVER MOUNTAINS TO THE OCEAN
I'VE FINALLY FOUND THE ANSWERS THAT I NEED

ALL.

ALL OF THE ANSWERS
THAT WE NEED

END OF PLAY

Also by
Kristin Walter...

The Elves and the Shoemaker

Hansel & Gretel

The Last of the Dragons

The Selfish Giant

www.ingramcontent.com/pod-product-compliance
Lightning Source LLC
Chambersburg PA
CBHW061056050726
47592CB00004B/1707